BETTER CALL BATMAN!™

adapted by J. E. Bright   illustrated by Patrick Spaziante
based on the screenplays *Animal Instincts* and *Monster Mayhem*
written by Heath Corson
Batman created by Bob Kane with Bill Finger

Ready-to-Read

Simon Spotlight
New York   London   Toronto   Sydney   New Delhi

Based on the screenplays by Heath Corson

Copyright © 2016 DC Comics.
BATMAN and all related characters and elements © & ™ DC Comics and Warner Bros. Entertainment Inc. (s16)

SIMON SPOTLIGHT
An imprint of Simon & Schuster Children's Publishing Division
1230 Avenue of the Americas, New York, New York 10020
This Simon Spotlight edition December 2016. All rights reserved, including the right of
reproduction in whole or in part in any form. SIMON SPOTLIGHT, READY-TO-READ,
and colophon are registered trademarks of Simon & Schuster, Inc.
For information about special discounts for bulk purchases, please
contact Simon & Schuster Special Sales at 1-866-506-1949 or
business@simonandschuster.com.
Manufactured in the United States of America 1116 LAK
10 9 8 7 6 5 4 3 2 1
ISBN 978-1-4814-7956-1 (hc)
ISBN 978-1-4814-7955-4 (pbk)
ISBN 978-1-4814-7957-8 (eBook)

Batman and the heroes protect Gotham City. The city is full of bad guys, and bad guys are full of surprises!

Cheetah has lightning speed and razor-sharp claws. When she breaks into a jewelry store, Nightwing is there to stop her.

"I'll make this fast," Nightwing says.
"You don't know fast," she says.
She pounces and swipes her claws.

Killer Croc bursts through the floor. He has metal jaws and super-strength.

"You started without me," he whines to Cheetah. Together they escape.

Cheetah and Killer Croc join the
Penguin's team.
"Ah, my animal allies!" he says.

The Penguin is a super-villain.
He plans to take over Gotham City
with his army of Cyber Animals.

"This will be a night to remember!"
the Penguin squawks.
Only Batman can stop him now.

Batman and the heroes
reprogram the Cyber Animals.
Now they are under Batman's
control!

"No!" the Penguin cries.
He is helpless without his gadgets.
"Ta-ta!" he says as he flees.

The Gotham City police take away the Penguin's team. "You can't keep me locked up like an animal!" cries Cheetah. Sadly, she is right.

Bad guys are kept at Arkham Asylum, but they often break out. Solomon Grundy does just that. He punches through the wall and runs into the night. He is strong but not very smart.

"Come on!" he shouts as he escapes.

Silver Banshee is a spooky villain. She has a supersonic scream.
"Hold up, Grundy. I'm coming!" she replies.

Together the bad guys have fun.
"Faster!" Solomon Grundy shouts.
"Take the wheel," Silver Banshee
says. She screams to stop the police
from chasing them.

Scarecrow is a smart and scary villain. He uses fear gas on his enemies. When he sees Solomon Grundy and Silver Banshee, he ends their joyride.

"I'll drive," Scarecrow says. Trouble is brewing in Gotham City, and he doesn't want to be late to the party.

Across town Clayface makes mayhem. He changes his shape to look like a dinosaur!
"Roar!" he says, scaring the people at the museum.

Clayface joins the other bad guys.
They are working for a big, bad
boss with a big, bad plan!

Their boss is the Joker, a
super-villain also known as
the Clown Prince of Crime.
He plays jokes to spread mayhem in
Gotham City. He is Batman's
worst enemy.

The bad guys take over the city with a computer virus.
"I am now king of Gotham City!" the Joker says.

The Joker won't rule long. Batman has a king-size plan to stop this king-size clown.

First the Gotham City police trick
Solomon Grundy.
"No!" he yells as he falls
through a trapdoor.

Next Green Arrow uses knockout
gas on Silver Banshee. Now she
can't use her supersonic scream.

Then Nightwing sneaks up behind
Scarecrow.
"Boo!" Nightwing says and stuns
him with his electric clubs.

Finally Red Robin throws cement on Clayface. "I'll crush you!" Clayface says as he hardens in place.

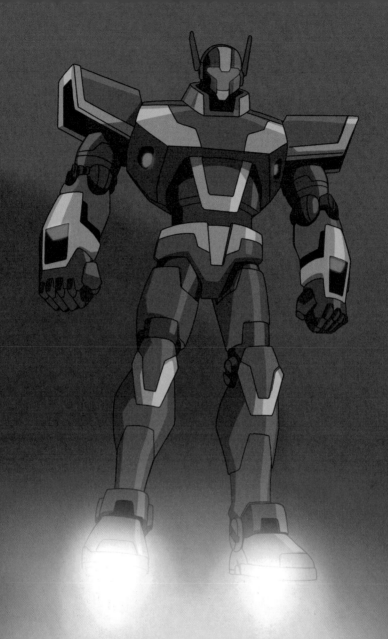

The Joker has a trick up his sleeve.
"Like the suit? It's new!" he says.
He laughs as he flies away in his
rocket-powered suit.

Batman thinks fast.
He takes off in a fighter plane
from the museum.

Batman battles the Joker in the sky.
The Joker crashes and disappears.

The city goes back to normal for now.
Batman wonders when the Joker

For the bad guys, there is always a next time. For Gotham City, Batman will always answer the call.

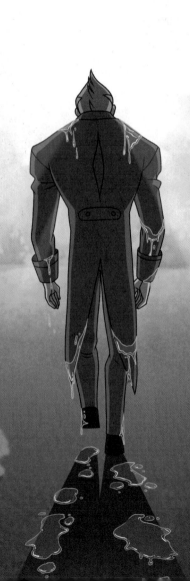